Daisy and Maisie

and the

Great

Lizard Hunt

Daisy and Maisie and the Great Lizard Hunt
Text copyright © 2015 Connie Shelton
Illustrations by Tran Xuan Duc - CloudPillow Studio,
copyright © 2015 Columbine Publishing Group

Daisy and Maisie and all related characters are trademarked ™ and ©
by Columbine Publishing Group

Printed in the United States of America

ISBN-13: 978-1517664534
ISBN: 1517664535

First paperback edition: October, 2015

Published by Secret Staircase Books, an imprint of Columbine Publishing Group
PO Box 416, Angel Fire, NM 87710 USA

Daisy and Maisie

and the

Great
Lizard Hunt

WRITTEN BY CONNIE SHELTON

ILLUSTRATED BY TRAN XUAN DUC

Daisy is a yellow puppy. She has a big sister, Maisie, who is six years old. They both live with their person, Dan. They live at the edge of the desert in Arizona.

Daisy loves to hunt lizards in the desert. They run so fast! She runs really fast, too. Usually she can't catch them. It is fun to try, though.

One day, Daisy and Maisie and Dan were walking from their house toward the river. Dan let the dogs race ahead.

"Don't go too far," Dan shouted to the dogs.

Just ahead, Daisy spotted a lizard. It was standing still! She lunged at it.

Her front feet landed right where . . . the lizard used to be.

He had zipped away.

There he was again, only a few feet from her! Daisy jumped over a sage bush. But the lizard was gone again. Daisy turned to look for Maisie but Maisie was far behind.

She saw another lizard. He stood on a sand dune near the river.

Daisy let out a puppy yip. She chased this lizard. All at once the ground began to slide under her feet. She rolled over and over. She landed beside the water and looked up, feeling a little embarrassed.

Behind her, Daisy heard Dan's voice and Maisie's bark. Dan was calling her name. She jumped up and ran to the riverbank.

"I'm okay," she said to them with two quick barks.

Maisie gave Daisy a patient, adult-dog stare. Daisy caught sight of another lizard. She raced toward it. It disappeared into another bush.

A wiggle in the bush caught her attention. Daisy got ready to spring at the lizard.

But the wiggle was not from a lizard. Beside the bush was a snake! Its tail shook and made a rattling sound.

Daisy felt the hair on her neck stand up.
This was not a nice creature like the lizard.
This one meant danger!

"Daisy! Come! Now!" shouted Dan.

Daisy felt frozen in place.

The snake stared at her. She could not take her eyes from it.

Suddenly, a rock landed beside the snake. Its body turned quickly and it disappeared into the bush.

Daisy looked toward her family. Dan had thrown the rock. She felt so happy that she ran right to him. He clipped the leash to her collar.

"Daisy, it pays to be patient and go slowly," he said.

Maisie sniffed Daisy's neck and licked her face.

"I was so worried about you," she told Daisy with a doggie whimper.

"I wasn't really afraid," Daisy said. She perked up her ears to prove it.

Maisie nipped at Daisy's ear with her teeth. "You should listen to Dan. You could have been hurt."

Daisy looked down. Maisie was right. She really had been scared. She should have looked carefully at the bush before jumping toward it.

Daisy and Maisie trotted beside Dan all the way home. When they went inside, each dog got a big cookie.

Then Daisy fell asleep on the rug by the fireplace. It had been a very adventurous day.

Follow Daisy and Maisie on even more adventures!

Coming soon--***Daisy and Maisie and the Lost Kitten***

Visit their website

DaisyandMaisie.com

and the author's website

connieshelton.com

Connie Shelton is the *USA Today* bestselling author of two cozy mystery series for grownups, in addition to the Daisy and Maisie early-reader children's books. She and her husband live in New Mexico with their two dogs, the real-life Daisy and Missy (who graciously allowed her name to be changed for rhyming purposes in these stories).

Made in the USA
San Bernardino, CA
30 August 2018